How to Have a Great Day at the Beach!

Terrie Sizemore

DEDICATION:

To my dear sister,
Cheryl
Who we call Sherri

Foreword

You may be asking yourself *Why you would want to read a book about having a great day at the beach when you don't plan on going to any beach now or at any time.*

Great question. I would ask that too, but this little book may just inspire *you* to make great plans to have great and fun day doing just about anything today or soon, I hope.

IT'S NOT
WHAT WE HAVE
BUT WHO WE HAVE

1

Today is an ordinary day - or so I thought. I'm basking in Florida's warm weather. The sun's up early and I make sure I get my outdoor chores done before the really hot weather and higher humidity sets in. This happens at about 10 am. So, I better hustle.

I finished yard chores which consist of weeding my daily areas and picking up large sticks I don't want run over by the mower blades when I cut grass. I cleaned the ducks' pen too. Actually, it's my goose's pen as well. I have one goose and five ducks. All girls.

I never thought I could love a goose as much as I love Gertie. A friend called to ask if I wanted her. I said *Yes.* When I picked her up, she was sitting on a nest she was neatly arranging. I thought she was so cute as she took one piece of straw and brought it around her and her eggs. She did this again and again.

Amazingly, she allowed me to pick her up and put her in a large carrier to take her home. She talked and talked. Then, my friend and I gathered the nest and the biggest eggs I

have ever seen and placed everything on a tarp. We placed the tarp with her nest and Gertie in her carrier on the back of my truck. We covered the nest and eggs with another tarp.

When we all got home, I put Gertie's nest in her pen and she and her eggs were home. She has been the sweetest goose since. She follows me everywhere I go in the yard as I do chores and tidy things. She lets me pick her up whenever I want to and she lets me kiss her. There is no boy goose, so her eggs are treats for my dogs when I scramble them. Yum for them!

Gertie was lonely, so I found some female ducks and they're all a family now. They know I'm 'mom' and they all run to me for worms - a delicious treat for ducks and geese.

After my outdoor chores, I exercise. I do stretch exercises three times a week and ride my bicycle for forty minutes twice a week. Sometimes I think the yard and house work should be enough, but I push myself.

I check the internet for my mail and things I find interesting. Today, I laughed at a joke I thought was pretty funny — let me share —

I really do have a strange sense of

humor.

Then, it's time for breakfast. What shall we make today? I wish I had a bowl full of donut holes or I could have a hot-fudge sundae or banana split. My sister would think this is terrible.

BUT, I don't want to waste what's in my fridge, so I decide on avocado toast. I buy small individual cups of guacamole so the 'guac' doesn't spoil. I really hate when guacamole turns brown. They say - not sure who 'they' actually are - but they say it's not 'bad,' just discolored from that beautiful avocado green and yellow color I've become accustomed to. In any event, the small cups prevent that dilemma.

Unenthusiastically, I pop my all-grain, low-carb bread in the toaster. I remove the plastic over the cup of guacamole and scoop out my nutritious breakfast. Other times I cut up an avocado, add cherry tomatoes, olive oil, and lemon juice for my healthy breakfast. When the toast pops up - perfectly toasted - not too light, not too dark - I spread my guacamole and enjoy!

Next, I cruise the channels for something worth watching. Nothing interesting today, it seems. While surfing channels, I come across a rom-com I've seen at least one hundred times. No, I think I'll do a crime series I've been catching up on. Still boring. It seems like all the 'tele' has to offer are re-runs. To be honest, haven't most of us seen everything on that 'boob-tube' about a million times? Then, I happen to find some cartoons I hate to admit I love. They are creative and funny – that road runner being chased by that coyote and Tom and Jerry antics crack me up, even at my age.

I wish I could tear myself away from the tele and do something fun. As I sit on the couch, my mind begins to wonder what I would do today if I could do *anything*? I remember the trips my brother and I took to the Florida Keys. Great times. I would *love* to go again but dismiss the want to when I think of the seven-hour drive. Ugh! It's a long way down there. One would think it would be close because it's Florida, but it's over three hundred and fifty miles.

Then, I think lunch in Paris sounds nice. That's ridiculous. I can't do that today and be back for dinner and in time to put the birds safely away. And, I don't even have a passport. That would make world-travel a little difficult for sure.

I look around the house. I could sew something new. I have several embroidery projects sitting on the table in front of my couch. '*No*,' I better keep thinking. What about a new watercolor? That would be great, but I'm running out of places to put my art and have sufficiently inflicted my art on all my friends and family. They probably don't have anywhere to put it either. They're too nice to tell me so as well.

I keep thinking of things to do with

this lovely day. A bicycle ride to the springs might be nice. Maybe I'll check the local listings for new movies. If I still had a horse, I could ride. There are some paths between the houses where I live that are cozy through the woods and a nice place to just walk along on the back of a beautiful horse without the aggravation of others and traffic. I scrap that idea too because I am currently without a horse. I never thought I would be, but I am.

What about cooking? I find different recipes in magazines and collect them to enjoy *someday*. Today's not that day, unfortunately. I'm in no mood it seems.

To avoid such confusion, I should make a list of what to do when I don't know what to do. Then, suddenly, the phone rings! "Thank goodness. Come to my rescue, whoever this is," I say to myself. "Hello," I answered.

"What are you doing?" she asks.

"Not much," I tell her all I've accomplished this morning and bore her with chatter about my choice of breakfast. I tell her what I've been thinking about and my entire mental list of what I *could* do today. She laughs when I mention lunch in Paris. "There's nothing on the tube, as usual," I conclude.

"Want to go to the beach?" she asks in a playful, *I know you do*, way she does.

"For sure!" I say. I'm so excited I want to jump in the truck and head east to the beach. What a great idea!!! BUT I have to prepare.

"I'll pick you and everyone up in about

twenty minutes," she offers.

"I'll be ready!" I'm practically shouting.

We hang up, and I rush to get my things together. *NOW* it will be a great day!

And by *everyone*, she means the lady who wears a blue baseball cap and the *younger than us* girl who came to live with the lady who wears the blue baseball cap.

2

I settle everyone at my house before I leave for most of the day. I need to hurry to get things done, she's on her way. The first thing I do is let the dogs out. I watch them play for about ten minutes. The dogs are still puppies so they get that extra energy out and then they'll sleep while I'm gone.

Then, I make sure there's enough fresh water and food set out for the ducks. I give them pelleted food and those dried worms I mentioned. A friend once told me I could grow my own worms, but the thought of wiggling, disgusting creatures touching my hands grosses me out to the point I can't stand it. So, the best decision I can make for all of us is to buy the dried worms the local store sells. Problem solved.

Once the animals are taken care of, I change into my bathing suit. I wear shorts over my suit, because it's easier than changing at the beach. I have three different suits to choose from.

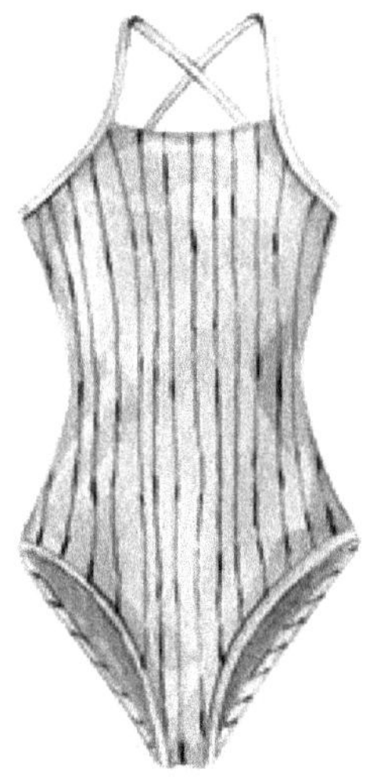

Today, I decided to wear my one-piece in case the waves are high enough to boogie-board. With the one-piece there's no chance of losing my suit in rough surf. That's happened before.

Next, I find my sun block. In Florida, we say we wear sun block every day that ends in 'y.' That includes 'today' too! I consider the SPF - code for sun protection factor - and, even though some say a level of protection of 30 is adequate, I don't think so. I heard an SPF of 15 blocks 93% of UVB rays from the sun and 30 blocks 97%. That is possibly adequate in other climates, but in Florida, where the sun seems to sit right on us, I prefer the maximum protection. Even though no sunscreen can protect 100%, I use 110 SPF sunscreen and wear a hat. Sunscreen clothing is available, but I don't own any. Maybe I'll put that on my next Santa letter.

The lady that wears a blue baseball cap wears that cap because she had skin cancer removed. Everyone who spends time outside in Florida is at risk for skin cancer, so we take it very seriously. I, too, have sadly had 'pre-cancerous' lesions cared for.

The lady that we're meeting at the beach – who wears a big hat - has also had some skin concerns. So, we bring our sunscreen and make sure we don't forget our ears as we cover our faces and arms and legs with our protection!

I pack dry clothes to change into after we swim. Thankfully, there are showers at the beach for us to rinse the salt water we love so much off. I pack shampoo as well to remove the salt water from my hair.

Next, I bring my sunglasses. My sunglasses are always a topic of conversation because I change them up each time we go to the beach. Today, I'm taking my oversized, clown glasses I think are so funny. They have UV protection in the shaded glass - which is actually plastic in these sunglasses.

We all have our own style when it comes to sunglasses. She has plain sunglasses, but the lady that wears a blue baseball cap has big, thick sunglasses that we call 'Jackie O' glasses because they look just like the ones Jackie Kennedy-Onassis wore. The young girl who lives with the lady who wears a blue baseball cap wears fashionable wire-framed sunglasses. She likes the 'hippy' look we say. The lady who wears the big hat that meets us at the beach wears fashionable sunglasses that look like that lady who played in Breakfast at Tiffany's. Everyone remembers her name but me. I'll change to my RayBans at the beach.

Sunglasses are 'standard equipment' in Florida. Friends I left in another state poke fun at

me, however, I tell them 'standard equipment'

in Florida consists of sunglasses for sure, water shoes, masks, snorkels, and fins, underwater cameras, wetsuits, kayaks, quality non-water cameras with zoom lenses, binoculars - not only those little opera-type ones, but long-range ones as well, beach umbrellas, beach chairs, and boogie boards. I have no idea what Florida boaters require.

She brings her own chair. A chair she's had for years and wouldn't part with. It's maroon and made for lounging - it has a long extension for her to prop her legs up and also has the usual cup holders on the canvas arms of the chair. She always hangs the carrying bag over the back of her special beach chair so it never blows away if we get a very strong sea breeze.

The lady who wears a blue baseball cap and the young girl that lives with her bring chairs for themselves and remember to bring one for me so I don't have to sit on the sand with my towel. They are sturdy chairs and have seen a little wear over the years. I think the salt air makes them age a little quicker than one would think.

The lady who wears a blue baseball cap also brings the umbrella. It's a rainbow-colored umbrella that helps us avoid those dreaded UVB rays we love to love but avoid as much as possible. We want our vitamin D but not that yucky skin cancer.

I pack some food for lunch, but the

lady who wears a blue baseball cap brings food and drinks for everyone as well. She likes diet Pepsi. The lady who wears a blue baseball cap knows this, so she brings two cans for her. Very thoughtful.

The lady who wears the blue baseball cap also brings diet Dr. Pepper for the young girl who lives with her and Mountain Dew for herself. I try to avoid soda, so I bring water in my reusable water bottle. I'm so perfect it seems hard for anyone else to compete with me! I remind everyone of this quite frequently.

We each bring bottles of water from home to rinse the sand off our feet when we finish our great day at the beach. This helps us avoid getting sand in our vehicles.

Last, but not least, I grab my biggest boogie board. We each have one, so we'll jam them in her van. I'm all set for the beach!

Now, I wait for her. She's picking up the lady who wears the blue baseball cap and the young girl who lives with her first. She'll be by soon.

3

Here she is! "Hi, all!" I say to everyone. They move over to let me climb in. I, my beach bag, cooler, and boogie board find a place in the back of the van. Don't be mistaken, the back of the van is still a place I can make my presence known.

"I brought my BIG board!" I say.

"We see," everyone says together and laughs.

"I want those waves!" I say, dismissing their laughter.

She likes oldies music like I do. And, by oldies, I mean sixties and seventies music. Simon and Garfunkel singing *America* is blasting over the speakers. This is one of my faves - so, with the windows down and our hair blowing in the breeze, she and I sing *"Counting the cars on the New Jersey Turnpike, We've all come to look for America!"* as loudly as we can. The lady wearing the blue baseball cap and the young girl that lives with her just sit quietly and listen. We know we're a long way from the New Jersey Turnpike.

When the song finishes, she turns the

volume down so we can chat.

"Which beach do you all want to go to today?" she asks. As if she doesn't know what

the lady wearing the blue baseball cap is going to say.

"Silver beach," the lady wearing the blue baseball cap quickly responds.

This is her favorite beach. There are beaches all along the Florida coast. Daytona is one of the most famous beaches, but so is Cocoa beach as well as others. Silver beach is just a hop-skip-and-a-jump from Daytona beach, but it's not as busy as Daytona beach. This is why the lady in the blue baseball cap likes it so much. She likes less people near us, but as the day goes on, more people will arrive.

Sometimes we join the lady who wears the big hat where she lives - north of Daytona by Flagler beach. The thing about Flagler beach is that the bottom of the ocean drops off more quickly there and is suddenly deep. This can be slightly treacherous if the rip currents are strong. The ocean bottom at Silver beach tapers slowly so we are in waist-deep ocean for quite a way off shore.

This helps us feel safe and the waves break at just the right place for boogie-boarding. I guess most like the beaches they're used to. We live here, so this is where we like to go.

Perhaps I'll get to some others someday. All of us - except the lady who wears the big hat - used to vacation in the panhandle. The lady wearing the blue baseball cap rented a cabin each year and we all met there. I flew in from Ohio.

The young girl who now lives with the lady wearing the blue baseball cap was living in Georgia. She would pick me up on her way down to the cabin. These times we spent at the beach were so special. Times one wishes would never end.

Our days in the panhandle were filled with rising early to run to the east side of the beach for the magnificent sun rise. Then we'd spend the day going back and forth from the cabin to the beach and, at the end of the day, we would rush to the west side of the beaches to see the sun set for yet another day. Our days were filled with good talk, fast meals, and rocking chairs on the porch for break time.

Once we saw a small owl in a tree and, like the tourists we pretended not to be, we took many pictures. Other times we saw dreaded poisonous pigmy rattlesnakes. Obviously, we avoided those.

And, when the time was over for that vacation, we all said *goodbye* until the next year when we would meet again in the panhandle for those great sunrises, sunsets, beach days, and time together.

As she drives the van today, we all have back-seat drivers' comments. "You better stop telling me how to drive," she insists. "I'll let you guys do the driving next time."

"But not the lady in the blue baseball cap," we all agree. She drives like we're on the international speedway Daytona Beach is famous for. We all laugh. It's good to hear our laughter. We are happy and are going to have a great day.

"Does anyone know the tide times?" I ask. It's important to know when 'high' tide is and when 'low' tide is for our chair placement on the beach. It amazes me how regularly the ocean 'comes in' and 'goes out.' When the tide is high, the water covers most of the beach

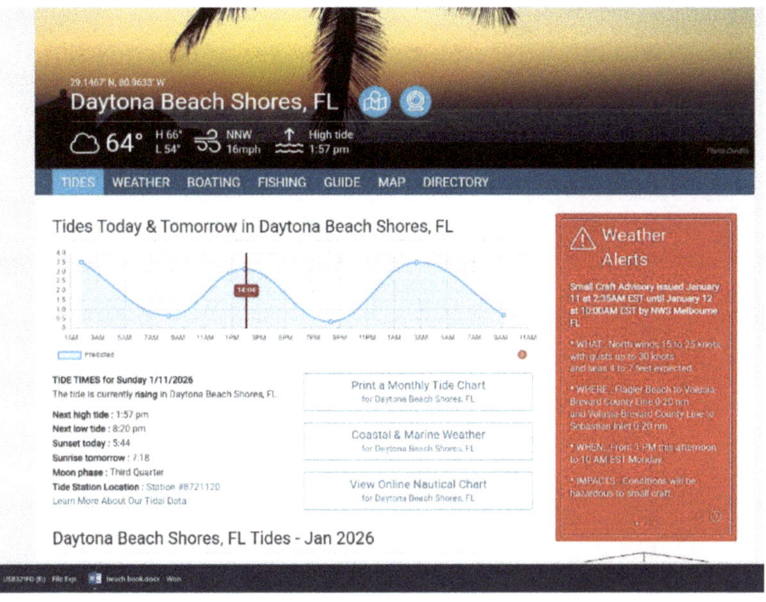

where we're going today. When the tide is low, we have more beach space to stretch out on with our umbrella and chairs. The lady wearing the blue baseball cap told me once about the tides in other countries and how they compare to our tides, but I can't remember what interesting tidbit she told me.

"The tide should be almost out when we get there," the lady in the blue baseball cap says. She checked on this earlier. She's a seasoned beach-goer, so she knows. She's the one who brings the umbrella that me and the young girl who lives with her will set up when we arrive at the beach.

"That's great!" I exclaim. "We can set up wherever we want to. Do you know if there are waves?"

"I looked at the webcam and the waves look promising," she says. "Looks like it's a good idea we all brought boards. Especially you," she says, looking at me in her review mirror.

She continues driving and we come to the high bridge over the intercostal waterway. I never knew this waterway is an inland waterway that is three thousand miles long and extends from Massachusetts all along the east coast to the southern tip of Florida.

Then, it follows the Gulf Coast to Brownsville Texas - wherever that is. The water here is mainly salt water, but when it combines with fresh water as it connects with other waterways, it's called brackish - a mix of salt and fresh water. It seems no matter how many times we go over this bridge, we are amazed at the engineering feat of placing this bridge across this waterway so we can be at the beach.

I love seeing the art on the sides of the bridge. It is sweet to me no matter how many times I see the mosaic art with whales, manatees, flamingos, sea turtles, and more.

As we cross over the bridge and, before we can talk about too many other things, we're at the beach! We'll continue our chatter after we get the umbrella up and set up our chairs. She finds a spot for the van and we unload everything and set out to carry our 'stuff' to the beach.

We're happy to find that there aren't too many others here yet. It's early and, for Floridians, not quite warm enough to frequent the beach. We love to start early. We are going to have fun!

4

It's a great day to be at the beach! The sky is azure blue and there's not a cloud in the sky. The rumbling of the waves sound like the ocean is calling us as always. The pelicans are gliding through the sky above us in perfect formation. Soon, they'll be over the water looking for dinner. There's a soft sea breeze coming across the beach making the hot sun a little more bearable.

We trudge over the soft., mushy sand with our beach bags and chairs and umbrella in tow. We find just the right spot. "This looks good." I point to our usual spot close to the ladies' room and showers. Everyone agrees.

Now we set up our chairs! She throws caution to the wind and sets up a little away from me, the lady wearing the blue baseball cap, and the young girl who lives with her. She likes to get *a lot* of sun. We know she's a sun worshiper and that's okay even though we know about skin issues in our climate.

"Good morning ladies!" The lady wearing the

big hat has arrived. She timed it just right. She's toting her lunch cooler and beach bag as well as her chair. And she's wearing her swimsuit as well. We comment on her 'Breakfast at Tiffany's' sunglasses and she has a big smile on her face as usual.

"Glad you could make it," the lady wearing the blue baseball cap says as she gives her a hug.

The lady wearing the big hat shows us her new chair. It's nice. It's made of dark blue canvas and has white trim. The arms are canvas as well and she shows us how big her new cup holder pouch is. We like when she shows us her cute new things, it's what's charming about her.

She's also toting a new cooler today. It is big and has a handle. "I packed lunch today in this new cooler. It's a little bigger than my old one." We all inspect the new cooler.

Then, the lady wearing the big hat shows us her new beach bag. Everything's new today! It has really big sunflowers splashed all over the outside of the bag. The rest of us look like poor folks with our hundred-year-old chairs, bags, and coolers. I like new and nice things too. The lady with the big hat is cute about all this.

Still wearing our respective sunglasses and having removed our sandals, we set up our chairs and the lady wearing the big hat and the lady wearing the

blue baseball cap sit and take sodas from their coolers. The sun warms us all as we sit in our chairs.

The lady in the blue baseball cap takes a Dr. Pepper from her cooler and hands it to the young girl who lives with her.

"Help me dig this hole for the umbrella pole," I say to that young girl who lives with the lady wearing the blue baseball cap. "We need some shade!"

"Sure.' She's agreeable and gathers the small shovel brought for digging this hole. We get to work.

It only takes a few minutes to dig because the sand is soft and easy to work with. The lady wearing the blue baseball cap brought water we pour into the hole to make the sand firmer after we set the pole and pack the sand around it.

In goes the pole and wah lah! We have the pole set and attach the top of the umbrella to it and open the umbrella. Shade. Welcome shade.

Today there's just that light sea breeze I mentioned. It's okay to have the umbrella up with a mild breeze.

Once, when we came to the beach, the wind was much stronger and all the umbrellas were having difficulty staying up.

The umbrellas flapped in the strong breeze and leaned over. Ours did as well. We even saw a couple umbrellas uprooted from their holes and bouncing down the beach, turning over and over. One day at this beach, the lady that wears the big hat's hat flew off her head because the wind was so strong. She was embarrassed. We helped her fetch the hat and she held it in her hand after that.

After a short time, I stand and say, "I'm going to check the water. Does anyone want to come?"

Everyone comes. We walk our bare feet to the ebbing and flowing motion of the ocean water. When we reach the water, it rolls over our feet. "It's nice and warm. The guard chair says the water temperature is at 84 degrees! Yeah! And a low rip today," the lady wearing the blue baseball cap says.

Rip currents are something we are respectful of. I would say we fear rip tides but fear is what gets you into trouble with them. I have never been in a rip before but the lady in the blue baseball cap was in a minor rip one day and she went right out to get her as I stood and watched. I admired her immensely for her courage to disregard her own safety to rescue the lady in the blue baseball cap. I am ashamed I didn't know what to do.

In any event, I have been told if you do get caught in a rip current, the ideal way to negotiate it is to swim sideways until you get out of it. People make the mistake of trying to swim into the current to try and get to shore. The current takes them out further and further and they are truly in danger when this happens. At least we don't have to worry about this today, thankfully. Each time we come to the beach, the lady wearing the blue baseball cap reminds us of these facts.

The flags they fly at the beach indicate there aren't jellyfish today either. Sometimes, we come and the jellyfish are wall-to-wall. They wash up on the beach, they sting us, and we just don't like them. Sharks are another topic, but I've never seen one and don't want to. New Smyrna is the place where sharks are abundant. We stay away from there.

We all return to our chairs and I cover my legs with a towel to protect my legs from the UV rays I love but don't love. We spend a little more time allowing the sun to make us sufficiently warm that we run right into the water.

5

"Who's ready to go in?" the lady wearing the blue baseball cap asks us.

"We all are." I speak for all of us.

We all get up and head for the water. I take off my shorts and leave my shirt on. It helps protect my shoulders from the beating sun. The lady wearing the blue baseball cap is wearing a special water shirt that also protects from UV sun rays. The young girl that lives with her takes her shirt and shorts off to swim in her suit with just sunscreen protection.

She also heads for the water wearing her suit. We all reach the water at the same time, but the lady who had the big hat on is the first to dive in once she's in waist-deep water. The rest of us are close behind.

The water is too calm to ride waves when we first go in, so we just play in the waves. We rise and fall with the rhythm of the waves coming in one after another. "It's calm right now," the lady who still has her blue baseball cap on remarks.

"This is my favorite ocean," I reply. I have been known to experience motion sickness and don't like taking medication for this. So, it helps if the water isn't too rough. Today, I can float on my back and ride the soft waves up and down and enjoy the sun beating down on my body. I made sure I covered my face and legs and arms with sunscreen. I covered my ears too. Many people overlook their ears and this is a mistake. The skin over our ears is sensitive and also requires protection from the sun's ultraviolet rays.

Sometimes the wave is bigger than I expect and it washes over my face. I taste the salty water and jump off the bottom to make sure I'm not in too deep of water. It's fun to have the water roll me around like I'm a rag doll. I think how lucky we are to be in this vast body of water in the summer sun.

The current divided us into separate groups. The lady who had the big hat on is swimming close to the lady wearing the blue baseball cap so they talk together about what they both did since they saw each other last. The lady with the blue baseball cap is pretty skilled at moving along with the gentle waves so her cap isn't swept off. She tells the lady who had the big hat on about her latest antics with her dogs when they went walking on a trail near her home. Then, the lady with the big hat tells the lady with the blue baseball cap about her new dog. She just found a little ball of white fluff and she and her husband have fallen in love. The young girl who lives with the lady wearing the blue baseball cap treads water close to these two ladies and just listens.

As everyone was splashing around in the ocean, she and I talked and laughed and floated in the water as the current was gradually taking us slightly north of where we started. We talked about past times at the beach and swimming. We talked about making more plans. We want to kayak the Rainbow River, take a few-day vacation to the panhandle - this time to a bed-and-breakfast in Apalachicola. We reminisce about our fun times there walking the small city, swinging on swings at the local park, and treating ourselves to ice cream. And never-ending small talk.

She shares her current art project with me - a beautiful picture made of twirled paper.

I know her work and am sure I'll love it when I see it. She also shared how she's been using resin to make small meaningful projects for people she loves. I can't wait to see these also. We talk about family and politics and wanting to visit the local museum because the one in Daytona has an Audubon exhibit. We both love birds and the museum even has a movie about bird migration.

"This was a great idea," I say.

"I know." She smiles. "Just what everyone needed."

"I was so bored and was so happy when you phoned."

"Glad I did too."

Then, she playfully puts her face in the water and her hand on her head – mimicking a shark! It's so nice to have someone who makes you laugh.

"Very funny," I say to her. "I am afraid of sharks. You know they're here. Remember when the young girl who lives with the woman in the blue baseball cap felt something really 'big' hit her leg? And we all got out right away?"

"I remember she says," laughing.

"I see the waves are kicking up, I'm going to get my boogie board. Want me to get yours?"

"Sure, we'll race on the waves."

"Does anyone else want a boogie board?"

The woman who wears the big hat shouts, "Bring mine, please."

"Mine too," adds the lady wearing the blue baseball cap.

"What about you?" I ask the young girl

who lives with the lady in the blue baseball cap.

"Sure," she says.

I walk out of the ocean and head for our chairs. I'm not sure how the lady with the blue baseball cap is going to manage to keep her cap on while surfing the waves. We'll see. She'll be alright for a few minutes without it, I think.

I grab five boogie boards and pass them out when I get close to everyone.

"Here comes a wave!" I exclaim.

We all position our boards in front of us, ready to jump on, as the wave approaches. There's that perfect moment when the wave arrives that we jump on to have it carry us to the shore. Away we go!! We all jump the wave and, with a rush, the boards carry us to the sandy shore.

"That was great," the lady wearing the blue baseball cap says. She kept her cap on too!

"It was!" I add. "Let's do that again."

We all hold our boards and head back out to where the waves break and can carry us in. It's almost like sled riding, but the waves are forceful and carry us without any effort of our own as we surf them. Sometimes we're pushed off the board before we get to the shore, but most of the time, we arrive at the end of the sea - where the water curls back into itself.

After about twenty minutes of riding the waves, we're all tired and need a break. We all, holding our boards, walk out of the ocean. We're dripping wet, but we dry quickly in the almost one-hundred-degree weather.

It's the awesomeness of the ocean that thrills our hearts each time we visit it. It's vast and different each time we come. Sometimes it's like a quiet kitten and sometimes it's like a roaring lion.

The ocean is something to be respected as well as loved and enjoyed.

6

When we finish session one in the water, it's lunch time. She doesn't sit under the umbrella with the rest of us, but she's close. She's a vegetarian, so she packed small snacks and fruit. She still has her diet Pepsi. I accept a sandwich from the lady wearing the blue baseball cap. I didn't pack much because the lady in the blue baseball cap always does. The young girl who lives with the lady in the blue baseball cap is a vegetarian as well as she is, so she eats snacks and fruit too.

The lady wearing the big hat packed a big lunch as she usually does. She has a thick sandwich with ham, tomato, and lettuce. She has small containers of cucumbers and chips for snacks. She tops it all off with diet soda.

As we all munch, we look over the beach. Perhaps we are catty. We comment on some bathing suits that show a little more rear than we would feel comfortable with. We also comment on some sunbathers who are in the direct sun on long beach chairs tanning. I cringe sometimes when I see this because of the - you know - skin cancer we are known for in Florida. The sun is wonderful but, like I said, it's close to the earth in our part of the world. Very intense.

We mention things about the folks walking by and some of the ones riding by. I wonder what others think of us sometimes. We talk loudly and laugh like things are the funniest things we've ever heard.

We make much over the sea gulls and sandpipers. We feed them bread we brought just for them as well as the lady in the blue baseball cap throws them bits of her sandwich crust. When the birds see the bread, it seems they come from everywhere to swoop down for their share. This always amazes me because there doesn't seem to be very many until the bread bag opens. We want everyone to have some, so we're careful to make sure one or two don't hog every bite.

We love those little sandpipers. Their little, tiny legs move so fast as they pick at the sand with their beaks when the water goes out, then rush away to the dry sand as the water comes back inland. They never seem to tire because they do this the entire time we're at the beach.

And I never tire of seeing the pelicans. They're fishing. I tried to get a photograph of them soaring above us but they come quicker than I can get my camera ready. I try over and over for the perfect picture of the pelicans as they glide through the air. Then, they make their way over the water and, when they spot a desired fish, they dive right into the water after it. Sometimes, they sit on the waves and I can see their little bodies rise and fall with the incoming and outgoing gentle waves.

It's nice to just sit on the beach and hear the water as it flows in and out. We're together and sharing ideas and thoughts as they come to us. Occasionally, we poke fun at one another. We do this in the spirit of just having fun. Each trip we take different shots at different people. Today, it's my turn to be the butt of everyone's chiding. A friend helped me move some heavy furniture and I promised to pay by taking her to lunch. When the lady in the blue baseball cap commented I should just take her to McDonald's I said, "She helped me move all that heavy furniture and you want me to take her to McDonald's?" The lady in the blue baseball cap realized how silly this was and shrugged her shoulders and pouted her lips, as if to say "OOPS!" Needless to say, we didn't go to McDonald's.

We recall other faux pas as well. Each of us makes a lot of these. I'm always glad that not that many people catch it when we blunder.

The lady wearing the blue baseball cap reminds us of the time we were at her home making pizza and I was recorded as saying, "We get away with murder when she's not home." We made a little bit of a mess trying to put the pizza together to bake it in the oven while she was at work. We laughed about it again. "At least we cleaned it all up," I interjected.

"Want to walk down the beach?" she asks, breaking things up.

"Oh, yeah!" I jump up, ready to walk.

We walk in the surf and see one of the many food trailers parked on the beach. "Want some ice cream?" she asks.

"Let's see what they have," I reply.

We walk over and can't believe the ice cream is almost five dollars for one orange popsicle. "I only have five dollars," she says.

"That's ok, I never bring money to the beach. I don't need ice cream right now."

The ice cream sure looks good on this hot day, but I'm glad she's the one enjoying it. I'll just wait to get home to eat some.

As we continue our walk, we go to the gift store to see what it has for us today. We love our little trinkets. This gift shop is the nicest one on the beach. It has music boxes, clothes, books, jewelry, wall hangings, cups, blankets, postcards, and more. She likes a light-weight blue jean jacket and buys it. She looks good in everything she wears.

We get back to our chairs after a little longer walk on the beach.

"Are we going back in?" the lady with

the big hat asks.

"I'm done, I think," I say.

She doesn't want to go either, but the lady with the blue baseball cap and the young girl who lives with her go back in for round two.

She and I just sit, watching them in the water and all the people walking by, riding bikes by, or driving on the beach. Everyone is having a great day at the beach. Us too.

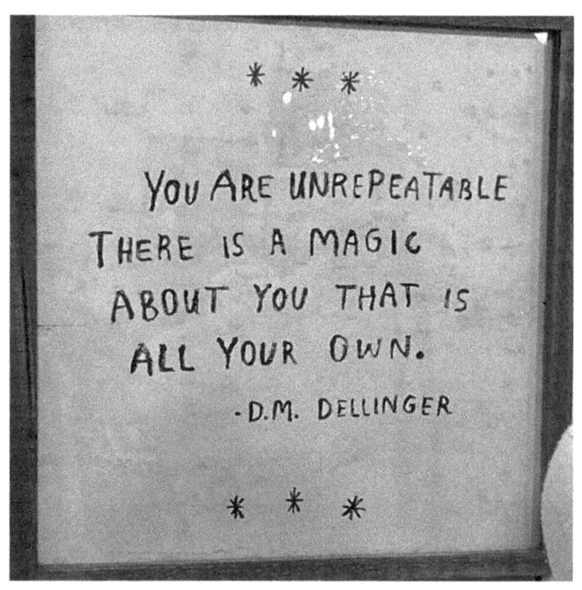

7

As we sit silently on the beach, I watch all that's going on around us - children splashing in the surf, boogie boarders riding waves, surfers on the waves out further in the ocean water, families carrying their little ones into the ocean and more - and listen to everyone, talking, laughing, sipping sodas, and soaking in the perfect Florida weather,

I look at her. She's so poised. I wish I knew the exact words to say to her about what I think and feel. I wish I knew the words to convey all my admiration.

I don't think she even knows how beautiful and brilliant and brave she is. She is smart and creative. All her talented hands do results in beautiful creations. I know her heart is happy to see her own work, but so is everyone else. She made a beautiful vase of shell flowers by gluing little shells on the ends of wire rods. She picked a beautifully fluted vase and added little purple flowers to make it complete. Spectacular.

She also made a map of Florida with all the fun areas she visited with family and when she was alone and used colorful items like flip-flops and flowers to add to the map that makes it special.

I like that she likes my art as well. She appreciates my art more than anyone else I share it with. It makes me feel like I'm an artist too. This is a great feeling.

She's easy to talk to and has deep feelings on life and things that I share deep feelings about. We are kindred spirits - very much alike. We share things about love and family and aging and seeing the wonderful things in the world around us. She appreciates nature and beautiful things the way I do.

She has been following politics all her life and I learn so much about my country that I truly should know, but don't. She served in our military and has always vowed to be a soldier. I may be older than she is but I look up to her. She is an avid reader and I wish every day I was more like her. She is truly a genius.

I wish I had thousands of words to say how special she is and generous and so much fun to be around. When I first came to Florida, she invited me to so many things. I never heard of Kenny G until she introduced me.

She loves flavored coffee and has been known to grind her own beans. She is a caregiver and has spent so much of her life giving to her family and ones she loves.

She is thoughtful with gifts that are meaningful and a treasure to embrace. A friend once told me life is a series of ups and downs, we need to surround ourselves with beautiful things. She surrounds me with beautiful things I will always treasure that remind me of her each time I look at them.

She appreciates movies like I do. Movies touch us both in almost the very same manner. She shared a movie about Ronald Reagan with me. It was touching. I was unaware of some of the facts surrounding his life, but she knows everyone one of those facts - and did watch the television coverage of saying *goodbye* to an amazing and wonderful past President and man of God.

We share the same faith in the God we love and call Him Lord of our lives and know the people we have loved and lost are waiting for us in heaven. She sees God for the Eternal One He is and the Creator of all the things beautiful and wonderful and amazing around us and in us. She lives every day to the fullest. As the Chinese artist's art captured the words, *Every day is a good day*. She embraces such things. It is so much fun to know her and spend time with her. Time is truly the only gift we have to give each other. Time is precious. Time spent together is how we make memories to cherish.

She is talented and works so hard to do

everything with perfection. Sometimes, I get sloppy, but she is never sloppy or half-hearted when she creates or works or cooks or loves. We talk about everything.

Many people in the world may never know the joy of knowing her, but I do and will keep her and this moment in my heart now and forever and ever.

"What are you thinking?" she asks with a puzzled look on her face. I've been lost in my thoughts.

"Just thinking about the most amazing woman I know."

She doesn't realize it's her, but it is. We make small talk about the azure blue sky without a cloud in the sky, the planes flying over the ocean to land at the Daytona airport and wonder where they have been and wonder if they're home or on vacation, the difficulty we think we would encounter if we rode bikes on the beach, how happy the others look playing in the water, what we're going to do when we get home, recent recipes, new art projects, and more.

I wish we never had to leave. I wish our day at the beach never had to end.

CELEBRATE ONE ANOTHER AS
OFTEN AS YOU CAN.

8

Well, sadly enough, our day at the beach has come to a close. As the girls come out of the water, they sit for a while to drip dry. It doesn't take long as it's midday and the temperature is in the high nineties with an index of over one hundred degrees. It's the heat and humidity we Floridians have come to know and love.

We discard our trash, pack our coolers with empty cans and plastic baggies that once held goodies, tuck away the empty chip bags, and fold our chairs and knock the sand off them. She collapses her chair and puts it safely in her canvas bag until the next visit to the beach.

The young girl that lives with the lady who wears the blue baseball cap helps me take the umbrella top off the pole. Then, we rock the pole back and forth to loosen it and remove it from the sand. We knock off the excess sand and place the pole and umbrella in its canvas bag.

We hug, tell the lady in the big hat what a great day we all had, we'll make plans for another day soon, and say our goodbyes. We all head to our vehicles and stow our things and head for home.

We agree making plans is the most exciting part of having a fun day. There are so many things to consider and so many preparations to be made. Years ago, my brother would ask, 'When's your next day off?' He would make plans; really fun plans.

First thing, of the many things to consider when one wants to have a great day at the beach or any other fun thing is – and is the easiest thing to do – is to decide what to do! Today, it's the beach. Any time is a great time to have some fun in the sun! Yeah!

Don't have a beach? Well, there's the park. Or there's a drive-in movie. There must be a museum close by or a library having a cooking class or writers' group. You can make plans to do anything, anywhere.

There are so many fun things to do here in Florida, so it can be a challenge to pick one activity over another. For instance, I love riding my bicycle along a bike path that leads to a spring in a town called Orange City. As I ride, I'm always on the look-out for gopher turtles and other nature wonders. I hope I never see poisonous snakes, but have seen them on the bike path and during occasional walks. When I arrive at the springs, my favorite marine mammals to see are my beloved manatees. One of my friends thinks

that manatees are *not* beautiful, but no one can convince me they are not gorgeous and wonderful. They fill me with joy just being around them.

When it's warm and the manatees return to the ocean waters, I settle for garfish – my brother's favorite fish. Their long noses and thin bodies are easy to spot in the clear spring run.

Another fun thing I like to do is taking a walk around a local wildlife refuge called Lake Woodruff Wildlife Refuge. I won't go alone for safety reasons, but I can usually coax a friend to accompany me and enjoy some exercise in the wild and wonderful parts of Florida. As we walk and talk, we count how many gators we see sunning themselves. Now, to be honest, I'm terrified of alligators. However, if they are very still and sitting a distance from me, I could pass as someone with great courage. Ha ha.

Also, along the walking path at the refuge, we often encounter many different fabulous sites. Once, I saw a wood stork. I didn't even know what these were before the lady that wears the blue baseball cap pointed it out and told me what it was.

That same day, we encountered some otters playing – cute and playfully splashing around in a little pond area near the walking path that also serves as a service road for the park workers to drive on. The otters are super cute when they dart around at amazing speeds and duck in and out of the water chasing or running away from or after each other. I'm sure I saw one watching me to make sure I was watching him playing around.

Another time, my brother spotted a kestrel in the sky. I had never heard of this fascinating little bird, but every experience was a chance to learn something new with my brother who I know was a genius. He knew something about everything it seemed. I would listen as he'd go on and on about the creatures and all the experiences he had.

I have also experienced the pleasure of seeing baby sandhill cranes. During one walk, a mom and dad sandhill crane came walking behind us unafraid because they are so accustomed to seeing people. As they passed, strolling slowly, I noticed the little yellow baby, called a colt, walking between them.

I regret leaving the house without my camera. Like I mentioned in the first chapters of this book, cameras are 'standard equipment' in Florida. One never knows what they will encounter on a given day. The camera captures precious moments forever. I may have this sandhill crane memory etched in my brain, but it would be awesome to be able to share the actual picture with all my family and readers as well.

There are many other exciting things to do as well. For instance, there are turtle rescues scattered on both coasts of Florida, aquariums, flower gardens or looking for beautiful wildflowers, shopping venues, an Audubon society with orphan eagles and other raptors, kayaking along the many rivers here, and many more, too numerous to mention, things to have fun doing.

I didn't always live in Florida, however. I know others who have seemingly lived in so many places I am astounded. I think that wherever we are, there are many things to do. My past life was in Ohio. Some ask, *'Where's Ohio?'* I would too if I wasn't from there. We had Lake Erie for water. It's not the ocean, but still fun fresh water with absolutely no chance of being bitten by a shark there. No whales, no jellyfish, no dolphins, and, sadly, no manatees either. But the islands are always nice to visit between the United States and Canada. There are also many amusement parks if you like to ride on rides. Not my thing, to be honest. I'm either afraid of the ride or they make me queasy. That's never a pretty site.

I raced harness horses at most of the county fairs. At the risk of sounding like a local 'carnie,' I love the County Fair! After unloading my horse, getting the equipment off the truck and the horse settled, and fetching the racing number, I headed for the fair! I loved seeing the children's crafts, the sewing and art contests, the pies, the vegetables, everything else, the 4-H animals, and, my all-time-fave, the fair food! For fairs close to my home, I didn't need to be racing to visit.

Some love the movies. A friend and I had a standing date each week to visit the local theater to review the newest movie whose arrival we were anxiously awaiting. Lunch was part of the day as well. Lunch could be anything from fast food, sit-in, picnic, or lunch we would sneak into the theater and enjoy during our movie time.

But today, we went to the beach!! How fun it was. I have so many friends who have never seen the beach. So sad! I first went to the beach when I visited New York City with my girlfriends. We all went to Jones Beach. The ocean has always been fascinating to me. You either love it or you don't. I love it.

The second time I encountered the joy of the beach was when I was given a great trip to Florida as a graduation present. The trip included the beach! We visited one of the eastern ocean fronts as well as the Florida Keys – a trip that everyone should put on their bucket list to do at least once if you are able to take a vacation.

It is breath-taking to see the ocean on both sides of the small highway you're driving on as you travel south through each Key. The seven-mile bridge is a modern marvel. There are small deer on No Name Key that touch my heart each time I see them. They are friendly and approach visitors because they live in the residential areas where the deer are cared for and protected by the residents there. My brother loved to fish and I enjoyed some swim time in the salty water as well.

And that's how you have a great day at the beach or a great day doing anything fun you find to do. We hope you enjoyed reading about our day and it has inspired you to GO HAVE A GREAT DAY DOING SOMETHING!! Every day matters.

About the Author

I am Terrie Sizemore and have been publishing and writing since 2008. I truly enjoy literature, particularly children's picture literature and children's books.

I wrote this small book to remind us all that every day is a gift and another chance to have an amazing adventure.

I am blessed to have family that has shown me how to have fun and had fun with me. We have created treasured and precious memories that will be with me always. I hope you are inspired to GO MAKE MEMORIES!

www.ingramcontent.com/pod-product-compliance
Lightning Source LLC
Chambersburg PA
CBHW040841010826
48978CB00012BB/853